A Gift For: _____

From: _____

Published by Hallmark Gift Books,
a division of Hallmark Cards, Inc.,
Kansas City, MO 64141
Visit us on the Web at www.Hallmark.com.

Editor: Jared Smith
Art Director: Kevin Swanson
Designer: Scott Swanson
Additional Color Work: Ramon Olivera
Production Artist: Bryan Ring

ISBN: 978-1-59530-454-4
SKU: BOK1180

Printed and bound in China
JUL11

TEAM TAE KWON GO!

THE TALE OF TAE KWON JONES

Written and Illustrated by Ralph Cosentino

Character and Concept by Scott Swanson

Hallmark

GIFT BOOKS

In a battle against time, martial arts master Joe Jones puts villains in their place!

But just when Joe starts to relax and put his feet up, his mom reminds him he has one more tiny little chore to do. He has to clean...

...the GARAGE!

"Ahhh! But I was going to watch the
Moose Lee marathon with Jack and

But a martial arts master's gotta do what a martial arts master's gotta do. Using modern-day technology, Joe calls the members of Team Tae Kwon Go for help!

Calling Team Tae Kwon Go! Come in! Come in!

"Calling Jack! This is a Tae Kwon Go red alert!"

Calling Josh! This is a Tae Kwon Go BIG TIME red alert!"

With the grace of a gazelle, Jack springs into action.

And with the force of a rhino, Josh races to help his pal.

The team meets at the Gojo to plan their attack.

The garage door rumbles and creaks open, sending shivers up their spines. But Team Tae Kwon Go is ready to face their ultimate challenge.

With the fury of dragons, Team Tae Kwon Go faces off against the mighty...

Roboticus Maximus!

Next, the team must use their best moves to defeat Char-Khan, the Samurai of Fire!

Equipped with cardboard boxes, the boys pack the blazing villain away for good.

At last, the young martial arts masters meet their final test of courage.

Can they defeat Spidoro the Monstrous Mutant Arachnid?

The boys dig down deep, summoning every last ounce of inner strength to defeat their titanic foe!

Their mission complete, Team Tae Kwon Go stands with pride!

Mr. and Mrs. Jones tell the boys they did uch a good job cleaning the garage, they ave earned a much-needed reward...

**...Pizza! And not just any pizza–
it's Team Tae Kwon Go's favorite:
Fortune Cookie Pepperoni!**

But a hero's work is never done, and Moose Lee will just have to wait, because it's time to . . .

If you have enjoyed this book
we would love to hear from you.

Please send your comments to:
Hallmark Book Feedback
P.O. Box 419034
Mail Drop 215
Kansas City, MO 64141

Or e-mail us at:
booknotes@hallmark.com